For Charlie, who is learning to count.

Bill Gillham

And for Harvey, who might learn to count one day.

Christyan Fox

First published in Great Britain in 2005 by
Frances Lincoln Children's Books, 4 Torriano Mews,
Torriano Avenue, London NW5 2RZ

www.franceslincoln.com

Distributed in the USA by Publishers Group West

British Library Cataloguing in Publication Data
available on request

ISBN 1-84507-288-X

Printed in China

9 8 7 6 5 4 3 2 1

How many SHARKS in the bath?

Bill Gillham
Illustrated by Christyan Fox

FRANCES LINCOLN CHILDREN'S BOOKS

How this book works:
• Read the questions
• Count the animals
• Point to the numbers

The youngest children may only be able to count from 1 to 3 but there's at least one of these numbers on each page. You help with the bigger numbers.

How many chicks hatching out of eggs?
How many lizards running round the table?
How many giraffes looking in the fridge?
How many pandas doing the washing-up?
Count the animals and put your finger on the number.

0 none
1 one
2 two
3 three
4 four
5 five
6 six
7 seven
8 eight
9 nine
10 ten

How many fish swimming in the tank?
How many mice dancing on the floor?
How many squirrels swinging on the lights?
How many piglets playing in the sandtray?
Count the animals and put your finger on the number.

0 none
1 one
2 two
3 three
4 four
5 five
6 six
7 seven
8 eight
9 nine
10 ten

How many kangaroos skipping?
How many baby elephants on the slide?
How many monkeys climbing on the frame?
How many camels in the sandpit?
Count the animals and put your finger on the number.

0 none
1 one
2 two
3 three
4 four
5 five
6 six
7 seven
8 eight
9 nine
10 ten

How many lions driving a bus?
How many crabs crossing the road?
How many chimpanzees riding a bicycle?
How many bears unloading the lorry?

Count the animals and put your finger on the number.
0 none
1 one
2 two
3 three
4 four
5 five
6 six
7 seven
8 eight
9 nine
10 ten

How many octopuses juggling oranges?
How many tigers at the checkout?
Count the animals and put your finger on the number.
How many swordfish on the fish counter?
How many polar bears in the freezer?

0 none
1 one
2 two
3 three
4 four
5 five
6 six
7 seven
8 eight
9 nine
10 ten

How many butterflies doing a dance?
How many rabbits hiding in the bushes?
How many leopards licking their lips?
How many gorillas having a picnic?
Count the animals and put your finger on the number.

0 none
1 one
2 two
3 three
4 four
5 five
6 six
7 seven
8 eight
9 nine
10 ten

How many yaks having a shampoo?
How many hedgehogs having a haircut?
How many penguins working on hair?
How many ponies having their hair dyed?
Count the animals and put your finger on the number.

0 none
1 one
2 two
3 three
4 four
5 five
6 six
7 seven
8 eight
9 nine
10 ten

How many seals diving into the pool?
How many ducklings learning to swim?
How many dolphins leaping through the ring?
How many crocodiles in the pool?
Count the animals and put your finger on the number.

0 none
1 one
2 two
3 three
4 four
5 five
6 six
7 seven
8 eight
9 nine
10 ten

How many parrots singing a song?
How many rats having a party?
How many bees buzzing around the cake?
How many zebras blowing up a balloon?
Count the animals and put your finger on the number.

0 none
1 one
2 two
3 three
4 four
5 five
6 six
7 seven
8 eight
9 nine
10 ten

How many sharks in the bath?
How many octopuses on the towel rail?
How many frogs jumping in the washbasin?
How many pandas in the shower?

Count the animals and put your finger on the number.
0 none
1 one
2 two
3 three
4 four
5 five
6 six
7 seven
8 eight
9 nine
10 ten

How many snakes in the laundry basket?
How many bats flapping around the light?
Count the animals and put your finger on the number.
How many owls on the wardrobe?
How many ostriches in the bed?

0 none
1 one
2 two
3 three
4 four
5 five
6 six
7 seven
8 eight
9 nine
10 ten